A Faerie Tale Romance Novella

THE
LILY GATE
a Retelling of The Frog Prince

by
HANNA SANDVIG

For my three princesses.

I may not be a queen, but you're still daughters of the King.

THE LILY COURT

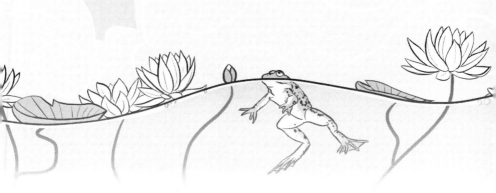

CHAPTER 1

IF YOU EVER MEET A TALKING FROG—any chatty amphibian, really—my advice would be to ignore it. That's what I should have done, anyway.

It was the most important day of my life. My eighteenth birthday. I was beyond nervous, so I spent the morning in my papa's industrial kitchen in France, making my birthday cake. Papa had been teaching me to make cream puffs, and for my birthday I created a towering *croquembouche*. I filled each little choux pastry with vanilla cream, then drizzled the whole tower with golden threads of caramel.

My mother had harassed me for taking the time to bake on such a busy day—especially when time runs slower in the human realm—but I didn't want to whip all that cream by hand. I needed the KitchenAid.

My human father was happy in Faerie, but he still kept an apartment in Paris. It was in an old stone building with a balcony view of the Eiffel Tower. There were rooms for my parents and me, and a professional-grade kitchen with all the shiny copper pots and cooking gadgets you could dream of.

Sometimes we came to Paris for a holiday, or to do some shopping, but more often, Papa and I just snuck off to cook. It was our own little world in that kitchen.

I put the last spoon in the dishwasher and glanced at the enchanted clock on the wall that kept Faerie time. Oops, I was running late. I pulled off the apron covering my green spider-silk gown and slipped into my satin heels. I didn't usually wear heels, but Mother insisted I look my best today.

"No one wants to see your bare toes, Tuala," I muttered in my best impression of my mother.

A glance in the mirror told me that pale pastry cream was smeared on my golden-brown cheek. I hurriedly scrubbed it clean and adjusted my golden tiara on my black curls. Good enough. Carefully, I lifted the platter holding the *croquembouche* and stepped through the pantry door that disguised a gate to the faerie realm.

Between one step and the next, the stainless-steel kitchen disappeared and I was back in the realm of Faerie, standing in front of the Lily Gate.

My kingdom's faerie gate stood on a beautifully carved stone platform in the middle of the pond in front of the castle. Pale pink lilies floated in the water, and stepping stones shaped like lily pads led to the shore. A stone arch, carved with lilies and gilded with the gold that powered the gate's spell, stood on the platform.

I heard the chatter from the party in the distance. Mother wasn't going to be impressed with me. I hopped onto the first stepping stone and wobbled on my stupid heels. The platter wobbled. The towering *croquembouche* wobbled. A little cream puff, right at the top, broke free from the threads of caramel, bounced off my platter and landed on the stepping stone.

I breathed a sigh of relief when the rest of the cream puffs stayed put. I had just gripped the platter more firmly and lifted my foot to step onto the next stone, when a little green frog jumped out of the pond and ate the cream puff in one bite.

I stared at it in disbelief.

"That was delicious! Could I have another one?" croaked the frog.

The frog was talking to me.

I stepped back in shock. Only there wasn't anything to step back onto, and I tumbled into the pond.

The pond was only waist-deep, but that was more than enough to soak me from my satin heels to my gold tiara before I managed to get my feet under me. I sputtered as my head broke the surface of the water. Little golden cream puffs floated around me and I heard a musical trill of laughter coming from a lily near me.

"Stop laughing, *sheerie*!" I hissed at the tiny faerie hiding in the flower. The laughter was smothered, but the lily still shook slightly. Of all the *aos sidhe*—the small folk—no one loved mischief like the twinkling *sheerie*.

The frog leaped from the stepping-stone with a splash and began to swim around me, munching three more cream puffs before the little pastries became waterlogged and started to sink.

"You!" I pointed a dripping finger at the frog. "This is all your fault!"

"I hardly think that's fair," mumbled the frog around a mouthful of vanilla cream. "It's not like I

14

tripped you. Those shoes were an accident waiting to happen."

"You're still talking! Why are you talking?" I gaped at the obnoxious amphibian.

"I should think I'd be allowed to defend myself against your ridiculous accusations..."

"No, I mean, why can you speak at all?" I pushed a sopping curl out of my face. My hairpins were lost to the pond, and my thick hair was already springing back up into ringlets. "You're a frog. Are you under a spell? Did you eat something magical? Anger a witch?"

"Well, Tuala, I—croak!" The frog shut his mouth in surprise. "Excuse me, what I meant to say was— *ribbit!* Hmm, it would seem I'm prevented from explaining."

"Interesting." I eyed the frog suspiciously. "And how do you know my name?"

"*Croak.*"

"That's convenient." I started slogging my way toward the bank. My bare feet collided with the sunken silver plate and I sighed and dunked under the water's surface again to retrieve it. My shoes I left to rot at the bottom of the pond. The goldfish could have them.

"It's hardly convenient for me," said the frog, breast-stroking along beside me. "I'd much rather be able to explain myself."

15

"And I'd much rather not show up to the start of the trials soaking wet and smelling like algae." I reached the bank and pulled myself up onto the grass, collapsing in a heap of wet silk skirts. "Looks like neither of us gets what we want today."

I eyed the billowing white canopies set up for the party. A row of low hedges stood between the courtyard and the pond. Maybe no one had seen my undignified dunking?

"I really did want to make a good impression today," I muttered, picking at my sodden dress.

"What's so important about today that has you all dressed up?" The frog settled down beside me in the grass.

I sighed. "Today is my eighteenth birthday and the first day of the trials."

"The trials?"

I leaned back on my hands. "Okay, so when I was a baby, my parents threw a massive christening party. Standard princess stuff."

The frog nodded encouragingly.

"And they invited all the heads of the Seelie Courts, and other important faeries, like Clíodhna, the elder fae. She came in disguise, of course, as she's still in hiding from the Unseelie Queen. But she did arrive, and she agreed to be my godmother. She told my parents she would give me the gift of true love.

16

She had looked in her enchanted mirror and seen that when I turned eighteen, they should hold a competition to find my future husband and co-ruler of the Lily Court. The winner would be my destined mate. My perfect match."

The frog flicked out his tongue and snagged a fly. He looked a bit shocked as he started to munch it. "What did your parents think about that gift?"

"As a Seelie princess, my mother was raised with a great respect for Clíodhna and her wisdom. She was very pleased."

"And your father? He's human, not high fae. What did he think?"

"How do you know my father is human and not one of the *Tuatha Dé Danann*?" Was this frog a regular inhabitant of our grounds?

"Well, your skin is a clue, for starters. The *Tuatha Dé Danann* are all pale skinned and your skin is golden brown."

I eyed my tawny hand and nodded. "But there are faeries from beyond *Tír na nÓg*."

"True, but your ears are also much rounder than is usual for a high fae."

"Fair enough, frog detective. Yes, my father is human, and yes, he was less impressed with Clíodhna's announcement. She insisted she had foreseen it in her enchanted mirror, but he was still skeptical. In the end, my parents came up with a compromise. They would hold the competition, but the prize would be engagement only, not marriage. Papa wanted to make sure I had time to truly get to know the person, before binding myself to them for centuries."

"Your father sounds like a wise man," remarked the frog.

"He is. He helped me come up with the challenges for the princes." I struggled to get to my feet. The silk dress was much heavier when wet. "And now, dear frog, I need to get changed. My mother is going to have my head for this."

"Really?" asked the frog.

"No, but she'll say *I told you so*, which is nearly as bad." I picked up the platter mournfully. "I do wish I hadn't destroyed my *croquembouche* though. I wanted to start out on a good note."

"But you're the one who gets to choose," pointed out the frog. "Shouldn't the princes be the ones who are nervous?"

"Logically, yes. But I still kind of feel like puking at the thought of meeting them all. Prince Naven from the Juniper Court was my friend when we were little, but I haven't seen him in almost two years. I've met one or two of the others at the high court, but I don't really know them. And a few are from other parts of Faerie, altogether. I wish I knew more about them."

"I see..." said the frog. "What you need is a—"

"Document detailing all their interests and character traits? I am working on one, but I don't have enough information yet."

"Um." The frog looked a bit taken aback. Not an unusual response when I started talking about research, but not an expression I'd ever seen a frog make. "No, I was going to say that you need an inside man. Well, amphibian."

I picked up the frog and held him at eye level on my palm. "I'm listening."

"I already have some knowledge of the Seelie princes because I—*ribbit!*" The frog grimaced. "And I could collect information on the foreign princes for you. No one would notice a frog."

I considered his offer. I couldn't deny I would feel a lot better with an ally to help me sort through the candidates. Even a small green one.

"Why would you help me?" I asked the frog. "What's in it for you?"

The frog watched a small dragonfly dance past. "I don't suppose you have any more pastries?"

I laughed. "It's a deal. Now, if we're going to be allies, I can't keep calling you *frog*. What's your name?"

The frog croaked at me, and then shrugged apologetically.

"Right, then. In French, you'd be a *grenouille*. I think I'll call you Grenie."

The frog sighed. "It'll do, I suppose. Now let's go meet those princes."

I helped Grenie up onto my shoulder. Even with my heavy, sodden dress, having a friend put a spring in my step as I walked up to the castle to change.

CHAPTER 2

WHEN I ENTERED THE COURTYARD in a pink (and dry) silk gown and leather flats, the chatter immediately hushed and everyone in the crowd turned to look at me. Princes, their doting parents, the various *aos sidhe* servants. I stopped and gulped.

"You'll be fine," whispered Grenie from his place on my shoulder, hidden in my curls.

I nodded and marched over to join my parents who broke off from the nobles they were chatting with to meet me. My mother walked awfully briskly for someone eight months pregnant. Annoyance gave her speed.

"Tuala," hissed my mother in a low voice. "Where have you been?" She picked a green strand of pond grass out of my black curls. "And *what* have you been doing?"

"Well..." I started.

"And where is the *croquembouche*?" asked my father in his Parisian accent. "You were almost finished when I stopped in to see you earlier."

"A story for another time," I said brightly. "Shouldn't we start the competition?"

My mother sighed and Papa gave me a look that said we'd talk about this later.

We walked together to the dais, shaded under a silk canopy. I scanned the crowd as we went, looking through the sea of unfamiliar faces for my old friend, Naven. Last time I'd seen him, I'd been sixteen. My family had spent the summer at the Seelie Court, as they did every few years. They preferred the quiet of our home at the Lily Court, but the King liked to keep a close eye on his nobles. Naven had danced with me at the Beltane Ball. One dance, but I had been thinking about it for two years.

My heart sank when I didn't see his blond head anywhere. It wasn't that I thought he was my true love. I wasn't sure I could love someone who liked to tease that he had changed my diapers—an unlikely story, as he was only three years older than me—but still, a friend in all this would be nice.

I poked the little frog on my shoulder.

"It's time," I whispered to him. "Keep a lookout for me."

Grenie nodded, and I turned to face the crowd. Everyone hushed expectantly. I glanced up at Papa, and he gave me a reassuring smile.

"Welcome to the Lily Court," I said, projecting my voice over the crowd as I had been taught by my tutors. "Thank you for answering our call to this rather...unusual event."

I took a breath. "I am Princess Tuala, heir to the Lily Court. This competition is to choose a suitable husband and future co-ruler of our princedom. There will be three trials. After each trial is judged, one prince will be chosen as a winner, and half of the contestants will be eliminated. Those who are not chosen may return home or stay on to observe the rest of the competition and enjoy our hospitality. The choice is yours. The champion of each trial will win a date with me, so we can get to know each other better, and a..." I hesitated and my mother patted my arm. She had insisted on this last part. Mother said there was only one way to know for sure, and it wasn't a list of pros and cons. "A kiss," I finished, feeling my cheeks heat up.

"And after all three trials?" asked a curly-haired prince from the crowd. "Is the winner of the final trial the winner over all?"

"Say *yes*," whispered my mother.

"We shall see," I said, wiping my sweaty palms on my dress. My mother sighed. I ignored her. "The goal is not just to win at any cost. The competition is a way for us to get to know each other better." There was no way I'd leave my fate solely in the hands of a game. I needed to observe the princes and collect as much data as possible to make an informed decision. "The winner will be announced at the ball next week. Are there any other questions?"

The crowd started murmuring, then a gorgeously dressed woman—doubtless a royal mother—asked, "When does the first challenge begin?"

"Immediately," I began.

The murmuring increased, and my mother clapped her hands together once, loudly. The crowd hushed and she gave me an encouraging nod.

"Immediately, after introductions," I finished. Ugh, introductions. I didn't love meeting new people under normal circumstances. And these were far from normal.

As the princes and their parents lined up, I adjusted my hair. Grenie croaked in protest, and I pulled a curl off his face.

"Any help you could offer would be greatly appreciated, frog," I whispered.

The little green frog leaned forward to observe the first prince in line.

"Prince Declan, of the Hawthorn Court," he whispered. "His mother is a bit...intense...but he's a good sort. He's in Crown Prince Tiernan's *fiann*."

"He's in a warband?" I looked at the tall, shaggy-haired prince dubiously as his mother marched him up to meet me.

"He is. Although it's possible he joined just to escape his mother."

"What are you muttering about?" hissed my mother. "This is not the time!"

I ignored her, swallowing the nervous lump in my throat as Prince Declan was shoved toward the dais.

"Prince Declan." I curtsied smoothly.

"Princess Tuala." He bowed.

"I hear you're a warrior in Prince Tiernan's *fiann*?"

"I am." He dropped his voice to a whisper. "Please don't send me home in the first round. I'll never hear the end of it from Tiernan and the others. Saoirse's been teasing me for the past two months about coming in the first place."

I smothered a laugh behind my hand. "I hope you're a good cook then."

Declan looked confused as his mother shuffled him off, another prince taking his place.

Grenie knew most of the Seelie princes, and it was much easier to make small talk with his whispered comments about their courts and families as they approached. We hadn't invited any Unseelie princes—can you imagine?—but six of the twenty princes came from beyond *Tír na nÓg*, their clothing and appearance proved that they were from realms I had only ever visited in books. I was a bit unnerved to think that anyone would travel so far for the chance to win my hand, even if they had all arrived through the Lily Gate.

The last prince was Seelie, and Grenie whispered, "Aodhan, Willow Court." But offered no additional information. The Willow Court was located down near the Seelie capital, and I was surprised Grenie had nothing else to tell me. He had known juicy gossip about all the other Seelie princes. Prince Aodhan came alone, although doubtless he had servants around somewhere.

"Princess Tuala, I'm so happy to meet you." Aodhan reached for my hand and kissed it with a bow. The prince was tall, even for one of the *Tuatha Dé*

26

Danann. His golden-brown hair swept past his shoulders, and his skin was tanned from the summer sun.

"Um, thank you?" I was flustered by the courtly kiss, and Aodhan gave me a knowing smirk as he rose. He held my hand for a beat longer, before I recovered myself and pulled it back. "Good luck in the competition." I had said that to all the princes, but I found I actually meant it this time.

"Thank you, princess." He turned to leave, then looked over his shoulder. "And Tuala?"

"Mmm hmm?" I pinched my arm. This was ridiculous.

"I do intend to win." Aodhan winked, then walked away.

I sighed and Grenie croaked in annoyance.

"You don't like him?" My pulse was racing. That one was getting bonus points for...I wasn't sure what. Did I have a category for winking?

"I'm apparently much less prone to swooning than you," grumbled the frog.

"I wonder where Naven is." I stood up on my tiptoes to scan the crowd. My parents had left me to mingle with the other nobles again. "He responded to the invitation. He should be here."

"*Croak*," said the frog.

"It was rhetorical," I whispered. "I know you don't know where he is."

"Your highness," came a gravelly voice from beside me. I looked down to see a brownie. The knee-high man was dressed in the pressed linen and wool of a castle servant. I recognized him from my time at the Juniper Court. The brownie held out a silver tray in his mottled brown hands. A folded piece of paper with a wax seal rested on the tray. "From Prince Naven."

"Why isn't he here himself, Forlagh?" I demanded.

Forlagh looked uncomfortable as he avoided meeting my eyes. "I'm sure I can't say, your highness. Please just read the letter."

I sighed and picked up the letter, breaking the wax seal of the Juniper Court. My suspicion grew. The flowery hand it was written in was not what I remembered from Naven's occasional letters. But he hadn't written to me in two years. People could change, I supposed.

Dear Tuala,

I was honoured to be invited to your competition, even if I have to admit that it's a bit of a strange way to choose a husband (I know, I know, you've told me all about the christening prophecy. But still.)

That sounded more like the Naven I remembered.

I was looking forward to seeing you again, but due to events I...cannot explain, I am unable to present myself to you today.

My heart sunk. He really hadn't come.

However, I assure you I am here at the Lily Court, and will be competing for your hand. I hope to be able to explain myself soon.
Your friend,
Naven.
PS. Feel free to ask Forlagh any question you might have. Forlagh loves questions.

I folded the paper back up. "He 'hopes to explain himself soon'? What is that supposed to mean?" I brandished the letter at the brownie. "Forlagh! What does this even mean? A note? Why is he not here himself?"

"Well...your highness..."

"Invisibility spell?"

"Umm..." Forlagh shifted uncomfortably.

"Did he grow a donkey's head?"

"Not exactly..."

"Infectious disease?"

"Not as such..."

"You may go." I sighed.

"Thank you, your highness." The brownie scampered off before I could accost him with any more guesses.

"Forlagh does not love questions," I murmured to myself.

"Oh, I don't know," Grenie said. "He seemed pretty knowledgeable. You should think of some more theories for him."

I narrowed my eyes in annoyance. "No more theories, my friend. It's time."

"Time?"

I climbed back up to the dais and clapped my hands in an imitation of my mother. The crowd quieted.

"It is time for the first challenge to begin!"

CHAPTER 3

WELL DONE, MY DEAR." MOTHER PATTED me on the shoulder. "I think you made an excellent first impression, even in those shoes."

I rolled my eyes. I had sent the princes off on their first challenge, and Grenie had gone along to spy on the princes for me. The competitors had been given four hours and the help of one servant to forage and cook a dish for tonight's dinner. They could only travel by foot or horse-back, no faerie gates. I had told them they would be judged on the taste of each dish, but really, it was more a test of resourcefulness and creativity. Two traits important to both a husband and a ruler.

Finally, I would get some data to judge the princes by. My notebook was ready to go.

The rest of the crowd had dispersed. Some would return home through the Lily Gate, and some would stay for tonight's feast. Which should be interesting, to say the least.

"I'm going to go lie down for a minute." My pregnant mother walked off toward the castle with a stately waddle. "Wake me for the feast."

My father and I watched her go.

"It's amusing that she believes there will be anything worth eating tonight." Papa raised an eyebrow in my direction, and I laughed.

"Not everyone is a trained chef like you, Papa, but hopefully they'll come up with something."

"Hmm, I have asked the cook to whip up a little snack anyway. Just in case," he said, then offered me his arm. "So, tell me, *ma chouchoutte*, what happened to your beautiful *croquembouche*?"

We walked together out of the courtyard to the gardens. The castle grounds were ringed with gravel paths lined with hedges. Fountains and pools dotted the gardens, all blooming with water lilies, with the large pond featuring the Lily Gate in the center.

"It was those shoes Mother made me wear. I slipped on a stepping stone and fell." I loved my papa, but the talking frog was more than I wanted to explain right now. "Cream puffs everywhere. The fish will eat well tonight."

"A tragedy." Papa shook his head regretfully. "I should have stolen one for your mother, while I had the chance. It might have been her only chance at decent food today."

"Perhaps I should have eaten in my room," said my mother four hours later, with a grimace, as she looked over the table of (possibly) edible offerings.

"Are you all right, *ma chérie*?" Papa fussed. "You look a little green."

Speaking of green, where was my spying amphibian? I glanced around the courtyard, which now glowed with candles on linen covered tables. No sign of the frog. Circling the long table, I flipped open my notebook and eyed the platters while continuing to look for Grenie. There were fish stuffed with herbs and mushrooms, a bowl of…was there a nice way to say slop? Minus points for that one. One plate seemed to hold a pile of moss. Things looked dire. Wait. An impressive cake dominated one end of the table. I drew closer to inspect the artfully arranged sugared wildflowers on top.

"How did he manage to bake a cake with foraged ingredients?" I murmured to myself, tapping my pencil against the paper.

"He foraged them from your kitchen." Grenie hopped out from behind a bowl of dandelion green salad.

"He got the ingredients from the castle? That's bending the rules more than a bit."

"Nope, he stole the entire cake from the larder, and threw some wildflowers on top of it." The frog hopped back up onto my shoulder.

I picked up the paper from beside the cake and read it.

"Prince Haldor of Álfheimr, you are going home." I crossed his name off my list with a flourish.

I circled the table, tasting anything that looked edible, and making notes. My father sampled some dishes with an air of longsuffering, but my mother declared that she would wait for the cooks to finish the actual dinner.

I gave high marks to three dishes in the end. Foraged root vegetables roasted with wild garlic by Prince Aodahn, fish baked with herbs and mushrooms by Prince Declan, and in a crystal pitcher at the end of the table...

"Is that iced mint tea?" I walked over and sniffed the golden liquid. "It is!" I poured myself a glass.

"A favourite of yours?" asked the frog, peering at my drink.

"Yes, especially if it's sweetened with..." I took a sip and sighed happily. "Honey. Perfection. I haven't had iced mint tea in ages. I used to drink it all the time when I was younger."

I picked up the label, written in the same elegant hand as the letter earlier. Of course. Naven. I flipped it over and read the note on the back:

In memory of the time we found the humming-bird's nest.

"Hummingbird's nest? Does that mean something to you?" Grenie hopped down to examine the note.

"You read?" I supposed I shouldn't be surprised, although it did add to the mystery surrounding my little green friend.

"I'm an amphibian. I'm not illiterate."

"Right." I laughed. "When I was ten, I spent a summer at the Juniper Court. My parents were busy..." My mother had been pregnant and lost the baby. The *Tuatha Dé Danann* lived long lives, but they didn't have children easily. I could see behind her current sharpness to how on edge she was with this pregnancy. I shook my head. "Naven was the youngest of six siblings, and the only one within a decade of my age. He took me out on adventures whenever the weather was good, and sometimes when it wasn't. We found a hummingbird's nest one day and spent the whole afternoon lying on our stomachs in a mint patch, watching the parents flitting in and out. We took some of the mint back to the castle, and the cooks showed us how to make tea. We gathered mint and drank iced tea for the rest of the summer."

"It sounds like you were good friends," remarked the frog.

"I certainly thought so. Which makes this all the more irritating. Why is he playing this game instead of just talking to me?" I crumpled up the note and shoved it into my pocket as I stalked up to the dais.

"Prince Declan is the winner of round one," I announced. "My congratulations on his lovely fish and mushrooms."

The shaggy-haired prince looked up from his conversation with another prince in surprise. I gave him what I hoped was a sincere smile.

"You may join me for dinner," I told him. Then I named the ten princes who would be going home. I heard some grumbling, most loudly from the cake stealer, but I ignored them. I ran my hand over the crumpled paper in my pocket.

Where was he?

CHAPTER 4

S O, PRINCE DECLAN, WHAT IS IT LIKE being a warrior in Crown Prince Tiernan's *fiann*?" I asked.

We sat at a little table tucked away in a quiet part of the gardens, on a circular patio with a trickling lily-covered stream around the outside edge. Little glowing *sheerie* faeries twinkled and danced around the flowers, uninterested in the discussions of the high fae. It was romantic and private.

Well, private except for the frog sitting on my shoulder, hidden in my dark curls.

"Do you spend a lot of time away from court?" I added.

"Ask him how many people he's killed," whispered the frog. I swatted at him, then pretended to adjust my hair instead. But Declan hadn't noticed, too busy trying to swallow his large mouthful of fish.

"Yes, we spend months at a time up in the north, patrolling the border between Seelie and Unseelie lands." Declan brushed his dark hair back from his face. He was actually quite handsome, tanned from a life lived outdoors, and broad-shouldered. I supposed I could do worse, although he didn't strike me as a potential co-ruler. He had the air of someone who didn't take anything very seriously.

"Ask him if he cuts his own hair on patrol. With his teeth," whispered Grenie.

I swatted him again.

"So many pests around tonight," I murmured. "Is that where you learned to cook? On patrol?"

"I picked up some things from Calder, who does all our cooking. He doesn't let anyone else do much. I think to keep Tiernan from ruining the meals with his 'help.'"

"The crown prince doesn't cook?" I speared a mushroom with my fork. The meal actually tasted pretty good, although I couldn't help thinking that I should have brought the mint tea along too.

"It's more that Tiernan shouldn't cook. He has a knack for making things inedible."

I laughed. I had never been around anyone who spoke so casually about the heir to the Seelie throne. Prince Tiernan, of course, hadn't been a candidate for my challenge. Whoever married him would be the future high queen of all the Seelie fae. I was happy to stay in the Lily Court.

"You talk about them as though they're your family," I remarked wistfully. I had spent so much of my childhood alone at our castle. Except for that summer with Naven's family at the Juniper Court and our occasional trips to the Seelie Court.

"They are," Declan said firmly, finishing up his meal. "I don't know what I'd do without them." He looked up with a grimace, realizing how that sounded.

"You don't actually want to win the competition, do you, Prince Declan?" I asked.

"I bet his mother made him enter," whispered the frog. "He looks like a mama's boy."

I reached up and flipped my hair, casually knocking Grenie from his perch on my shoulder. He tumbled behind me with a muffled croak.

"I...um...not really?" Declan answered my question, then scrambled to add, "I mean, you seem really...nice?"

"It's fine." I rose to stand, and the prince politely stood as well. "I'm not really feeling it, either. But I'm afraid we do have to..." I took a breath. This was so awkward. "We have to kiss. Or my mother won't accept my decision. She's adamant that it's the only way I'll know if someone is my true love or not." I rolled my eyes. "You know how mothers can be."

"Oh, I really do." Declan stood in front of me, and we both took a breath.

"Okay, here goes." And with that romantic statement, I leaned forward just as he did, and our lips collided awkwardly. I tried not to pull away too hastily, but he stepped back as quickly as I had.

"And what will you tell your mother?" he asked, nervously.

"That no magical fireworks appeared overhead." I laughed. "And what will you tell yours?"

"That it felt like kissing my little sister." Declan grimaced.

"It was nice getting to know you, anyway," I said. And it was true, I could see myself becoming friends with Declan, if we had more time together.

"Same. And thank you for choosing me for at least one of the challenges. Although I'm sure I'll be teased by Tiernan for a decade or so, regardless."

Declan left the garden and Grenie hopped up to me.

"Who knew it would be so tricky to find my true love?" I sighed, crouching to pick up the frog.

"It's probably because you have such violent tendencies." Grenie sniffed.

"Hmmm." I watched the prince disappear into the castle. I hadn't thought I'd feel so melancholy after one failed date.

"I know what you need," said the frog.

"Oh?" I looked at him on my tawny hand, his skin bright green in the twilight.

"Some mint tea. Let's go find it."

"That, *Grenioulle*, is an excellent idea." I forced a smile.

"And possibly some cake," he added. "For me, I mean. It might not be foraged, but it did look delicious."

"You know what?" I lifted the frog back up onto my shoulder. "You're very sensible for a frog. How do I find a prince with your excellent priorities?"

"You'll just have to see what tomorrow brings," quipped the frog, holding on to my dress as I started to walk back to the castle. "I'm sure your perfect prince is around here somewhere."

"I've had enough of princes for today," I told him. "Let's go find that cake."

HANNA SANDVIG

CHAPTER 5

THE NEXT MORNING, I STOOD IN A filmy pale blue gown on the far shore of the castle moat, my feet bare in the grass. The remaining nine princes were arranged in front of me, near the water. Well, eight princes. Naven was technically still in the competition, but although his brownie butler Forlagh stood in the crowd of onlookers, the prince was nowhere to be seen.

"Is this really a trial?" croaked Grenie from his spot on my shoulder. "Or do you just want an excuse to see all the princes without their shirts on?"

The handsome Prince Aodahn had indeed already taken his shirt off in anticipation of a swimming challenge, and threw me a wink when I automatically looked in his direction.

"Hush you," I whispered to Grenie, flustered, before raising my voice. "Welcome to the second day of the competition. Today's trial is a test of strength and speed." I gestured at the water behind me. The wide moat had no bridge. Visitors either arrived through the Lily Gate—with permission—or rode the small ferry across the water. The princes would be using neither.

"You will each be given a starting spot with a marker. When you see the signal, race to the matching marker on the other side of the moat. The first one to the other side is the winner, and the slowest five will be out of the competition. Any questions?"

There were none, and the princes began spreading out to the various markers. I had neglected to mention the giant water serpent lurking in the moat, but we had bribed Cressie with treats to stay out of the way. Hopefully the *peiste* didn't get too curious and come to see what all the splashing was about, after all.

"Well, Tuala, I must get to spying." Grenie hopped off my shoulder. "Enjoy the view!"

Yes, yes, by now the princes had all stripped down to swimming shorts. And yes, the view was pretty good. But that wasn't the point of the competition. There were more important qualities in a future mate than nice abs. Even though Aodahn undeniably won that test.

A couple weeks ago, one of the castle cats had a litter of kittens. Before gathering all the princes down here this morning, my mother and I had gently placed a kitten on a lily pad right in the path of each of the princes, close to the castle side of the moat.

There were spells in place to keep the kittens safe, but the princes didn't know that. And anyone who refused to rescue a kitten in order to win a contest wasn't someone I wanted to marry.

All the princes had found their markers, but the ninth marker was empty. Was Naven giving up? He had been given plenty of time to crawl out from whatever rock he was hiding under.

I threw a little golden acorn above my head and whispered, "*Léas!*" The acorn exploded with a shower of twinkling golden light, and the princes lunged into the water with a deafening splash.

I stalked over to the group of servants and found Forlagh.

"Has Naven pulled out of the competition?" I demanded.

"No, princess." Forlagh bowed politely. "He's competing right now."

45

"What?" I turned back to the moat. Most of the princes were only halfway across, but the stranded kitten in the path of the empty marker meowed as its lily pad glided toward safety. Only nothing was pulling it.

"Is he actually invisible?" I squinted, trying to see the water in front of the lily pad.

"Not as such, Princess," said the brownie. "And he wishes you to know that he's taking this competition very seriously."

"If the trial was to make me crazy, he's certainly succeeding." I turned back to the brownie. "Tell me honestly, Forlagh, why is he doing this? Why won't he just talk to me?"

"I'm sorry, Princess. He would tell you everything if he were able to."

"Come, Tuala." My mother put her hand on my arm. "We must take the ferry across and greet the victor."

I reluctantly let her lead me away from the brownie. He wasn't going to tell me anything anyway.

I stewed the whole way across the moat, trying to think of any reason why Naven would play these games with me. I pulled out my notebook and looked over my notes. I had been so optimistic about seeing him again when I started this whole thing. When we reached the other side where my father and a crowd of onlookers waited, I was no closer to an answer.

"So, Papa, who was the winner?" I helped my mother off the wooden ferry platform and we walked together to meet him. "Are all the kittens accounted for?"

"We're still waiting for all the competitors to finish. A couple of the princes reached the shore, and then went back for the kittens."

Not noble, but better than nothing.

"And the winners?"

"The first kitten arrived before any of the princes, if you can believe it. The lily pad came to shore on its own. Perhaps a spell was involved?"

"Naven's servant would have us believe his prince rescued it," I said with a snort.

Papa's eyebrows rose. "That does make things interesting. If he can prove it, then I suppose he's technically the winner."

"He'd have to actually talk to me to do that," I grumbled. "Who arrived next?"

"Prince Aodahn of the Willow Court," Papa said. "It was incredible, actually. He not only made it across before anyone else, but when he emerged from the rushes at the edge of the moat, he had both a kitten in his arms and Prince Bahadur. He apparently

47

came across his competitor struggling in the water and saved his life."

"What?" I glanced around, but there was no sign of the brown-skinned prince. "Is Prince Bahadur okay?"

"He was unconscious, but Aodahn kept him alive with chest compressions until the palace healers arrived. Bahadur might have drowned without his help. We hadn't seen him struggling from the shore. He was too deep in the rushes."

Aodahn must have heard us talking about him, because he looked up with a sunny smile. I waved back and walked down to the water's edge where he stood with a little gray kitten licking his face, his golden-brown hair already drying in the sun. I felt my heart melting and I gave the prince a genuine smile, my annoyance with Naven forgotten. My childhood friend wasn't the only prince in this competition.

"Princess Tuala." The handsome fae man patted the kitten's head. "I just had to rescue this little scamp. I didn't realize until the other princes arrived that it must have been part of your challenge all along. You're quite the clever game master."

"And you're quite the hero, from what I hear." I reached over and gave the kitten a scratch on the head. "I'm impressed you managed to carry both an unconscious prince and the kitten."

"I swim regularly in the river near our castle back home. Even with my arms full, the moat barely posed a challenge." He looked around at the group of princes, some of whom lay panting on the grass while the kittens wandered back to the castle without them. "For me, at least."

"Indeed." I did a quick count to ensure none of the other princes were missing, but everyone else was in sight. Everyone except Naven. I turned back to the handsome prince in front of me. "Well, I'm pleased to let you know that you're officially the winner of today's challenge. I look forward to our afternoon together."

"As do I," said the prince with that heart-melting smile of his.

My mind was so thoroughly in the clouds as I walked up to the castle that I nearly stepped on the little green frog hopping in front of my feet.

"Grenie!" I picked him up and set him on my shoulder, still smiling to myself. "I'm not going to need your help with this one. There was a clear winner."

"The prince who pulled the first kitten to safety?" asked the frog. "You saw that?"

"No, no." I pulled out my notebook and added some glowing remarks by the handsome prince's name. Clearly, he should get bonus marks for rescuing his drowning competitor. "I mean Aodahn. He not only saved a kitten, but he rescued a drowning prince as well, can you believe it?"

"It is rather…incredible," said the frog. "I'm not sure you can trust that one."

"What do you mean?" I glanced back at the prince from the Willow Court who was handing the kitten off to a servant so he could—sadly—pull his linen shirt back on. "He's been nothing but sweet to me."

"Has Prince Bahadur woken up yet?" Grenie gave me a meaningful look.

"I'm on my way to check on him." I tucked my notebook and pencil back in my pocket and started walking up the grassy bank to the castle. "Why?"

"I'd like to hear if his story matches Prince Aodahn's."

"Grenie." I pulled the frog off my shoulder and held him level with my face. "What are you trying to accuse Aodahn of?"

"Nothing you want to hear, obviously," muttered the frog.

"Say it." I narrowed my eyes.

"It's just that Bahadur was an excellent swimmer, and he was winning."

"Because he didn't stop for the kitten," I pointed out. "We had to send a servant back to collect the final kitten. And even strong swimmers can run into trouble."

"Sometimes that trouble has a dreamy smile and a strong desire to win."

I closed my eyes in annoyance. I would not fight with a frog. "Do you have any proof?"

"All I'm saying is that it would be smart to not fall for the first handsome prince to wink in your direction."

"Oh, so now I'm just a silly, stupid princess?" Okay, fine. I was fighting with a frog.

"You don't know him."

"I don't know any of them," I seethed. "That's the whole point."

"You know Prince Naven," pointed out the irritating amphibian.

"I don't know him either, apparently." I glared at the frog. "And come to think of it, I don't even know you. We only met yesterday. And you're a frog."

"I'm your friend, Tuala."

"I don't even know your real name." I set the frog on the ground.

"I'm trying to help you," he insisted.

"I've had enough condescending help for one day. Don't sabotage my date tonight, frog."

And with that, I turned on my heel and strode back to the castle.

HANNA SANDVIG

CHAPTER 6

I WAS STILL FUMING OVER THAT OBNOXIOUS frog when I got back to the castle, but I did stop in to see Prince Bahadur in the healer's room. He lay still and pale on the cot, and while the healers were confident he'd make a full recovery, his parents were preparing to take him straight home via the Lily Gate. When I saw him lying there, I felt shaken. I hadn't thought anyone would actually get injured in this challenge. I only wanted to test the princes' characters, not risk their lives.

I was subdued through lunch, as my mother chattered away about how she would trade a limb to eat a *beignet* like the ones she and Papa had eaten on their visit to New Orleans the year before. She had been talking about the doughnuts all week. Last week, she had been craving snails, and the week before it had been pickled fish, so fried dough was a step up.

"Tuala." Mother put her hand on my arm. "He'll be fine. Thank goodness that lovely Prince Aodahn came along when he did."

I smiled slightly. "That was very lucky."

"You seem quite taken with him. Aodahn, I mean." My mother grimaced and pushed her hand on the top of her pregnant belly. "Must you dig your toes into my ribcage, child?" she muttered at my tiny sibling.

I smiled for real. "I do like him. At least, from what I know of him so far. He's certainly ahead in points." Grenie's words still rung in my head. I didn't know any of them, not really.

"That's what this outing is for, my dear, to get to know him better. And don't forget, if you really want to be sure…"

"I need to kiss him. Yes, I know how you feel about it." I finished poking at my food and stood to leave.

"I only want you to be happy, my child."

"I know, Mama." And I did. Even though I never seemed to get along with her like I did with Papa, I knew she always wanted the best for me. I kissed her on the head, patted her belly to say goodbye to my unborn baby brother or sister, and went to get ready for my date with a prince.

Each of the dates had been designed by my mother for maximum romance and to go along with the theme of the challenge. The culinary challenge had, of course, been paired with a dinner date. The aquatic challenge led to a beautiful afternoon out on the water in a row boat. The cook had packed us a basket of goodies, and the moat gleamed in the afternoon sun. Willows trailed their branches while lilies drifted in the blue-green water.

Aodahn rowed us out a little way into the water, and then we got out the basket. We found glass bottles of iced tea (sadly, not mint), pastries, and strawberries carefully folded into cloth wrappings.

"So, Aodahn, I seem to remember that you have a large family?"

Aodahn took a swig of iced tea. "Yes, my parents and six siblings."

"That sounds wonderful." I tried to imagine growing up with so many brothers and sisters.

The prince grimaced.

"But no one came along to watch the trials?" I hoped it wasn't a sore spot, but I was curious. All the other princes had come with family members and courtiers, or at least trusted servants. No one else had come from the Willow Court.

Aodahn avoided looking at me and picked out a lemon tart. "We had a bit of a...falling out. Nothing serious," he hurried to add.

"I hope you're able to make up soon. There's nothing more important than family." I bit into a raspberry puff and searched my mind for something else to say. I'd never had much chance to practice small talk.

"This is an unusual way to pick a mate." Aodahn leaned back against the edge of the boat. "But I see the wisdom of testing a future ruler in skills of speed and survival."

"That's not exactly it..."

"And kitten rescuing?" he added with a smirk.

"Sort of..."

"There's more to it?" The prince tilted his head.

"Well..." I didn't want to reveal my actual reasons behind each trial. It would give him an unfair advantage in the final challenge. And I wasn't quite so sure about him anymore. There was something I couldn't quite put my finger on.

"Of course! It's not just about being a strong ruler." He snapped his fingers.

"Co-ruler," I pointed out.

"Right, right, but it's also about being a good match." The boat rocked and suddenly he sat right beside me on the bench. He put his hand on mine and leaned in.

This was what I had wanted, so why was I suddenly pulling back?

His lips met mine in a possessive kiss. My heart jumped, but not in a good way. I pushed my hand against his chest, but he didn't budge. I scooted back sharply against the side of the boat, forcibly breaking the kiss, but Aodahn just looked down at me with a smile.

"I think we'd be very happy together, don't you?" He drew closer again, and I turned my head.

"I don't think this is going to work," I told him.

Aodahn narrowed his eyes and gripped my hand more tightly. "What do you mean? I'll make an excellent ruler. And I know you find me attractive. I saw how you looked at me earlier today."

"Please back up a little." I attempted to pull my hand away, but his grip remained painfully strong.

All of a sudden, the boat pitched sideways. I yanked my hand free and leapt into the water as the entire boat flipped over. Scales brushed against my side as I swam for shallower water. I was grateful it wasn't far. Swimming in a long dress wasn't the easiest thing, even a light summer one. When I felt my feet touch the silty bottom of the moat, I turned to see what had happened to Aodahn.

Oh, of course, Cressie. The giant *peiste* had the prince by a leg and was dragging him sputtering through the water to the far side of the moat.

"Oh no, the ferocious moat monster!" I wailed loudly, hoping Aodahn could hear me. "So many teeth! I sure hope it doesn't eat you!" I finished dramatically.

"Are you sure?" asked a voice by my elbow. "If there ever was a prince who needed to be munched on, it's that one."

"Cressie is an herbivore," I told my froggy friend. "I'm just trying to make him nervous." The giant green serpent had stopped in the middle of the water and the pushy prince dangled in the air by his foot. He appeared to be alive by the amount of thrashing he was doing.

"That's what she told me," Grenie said, treading water next to me. "I suggested she chew off a leg or two, but she only agreed to capture him."

"How did you know I would need help?" I picked up the frog and started slogging back to the bank.

"You know I had my suspicions," said Grenie.

"I know. I'm sorry I didn't listen. I just...I guess I didn't want you to be right. He seemed so nice. And he rescued that prince and the kitten."

"When the servants went to find the missing kitten, it was the one on Aodahn's route. He never stopped for it." Grenie looked back at the prince, who had gotten his breath back sufficiently to yell out some very creative curse words at his captor. Cressie seemed unconcerned.

"So the kitten he rescued..."

"Was Prince Bahadur's. Aodahn realized his mistake too late. He would have needed to double back, and then the other prince would have beaten him. So, he took the kitten and half drowned the prince to keep him from talking. Showing up as a hero was a bonus."

I felt ill as I thought about how I had been taken in by Aodahn's charms. "I'm so sorry, Grenie." I looked down at the frog on my hand. "Thank you for rescuing me. You're a true friend. A prince among frogs. How can I repay you?"

"What are friends for?" the frog quipped as we reached the bank. "Although, I wouldn't turn down a raspberry puff. The pastries were the real victims here. Do you suppose there are more in the kitchen?"

"Let's go find out." I glanced back at the bellowing prince one last time. "We better send someone back to get him. And to make sure he leaves. Permanently."

CHAPTER 7

I SAT IN THE GARDENS THAT EVENING. The fountain twinkled nearby, and I could hear the murmuring and laughter of the party my mother had organized in the courtyard.

I wasn't hiding. Not exactly. I was going over my notes, and they didn't look promising.

"You see, Grenie, here's the scores for all the princes so far." I tapped the notebook open on the bench, and the little frog hopped over to examine it. "Aodahn was, by far, the best choice. He scored highest in all the categories."

"He certainly came out ahead in the category of entitled liars," said the frog.

"Very true." I sighed. When Papa and a company of guards had returned Aodahn to the Willow Court, he learned that the prince had more than just a "falling out" with his siblings. He had organized a coup and tried to take the throne from his older sister. Aodahn had been cut out of the family and banished in return, but if he was causing trouble in other courts, his sister agreed that stricter measures were going to be necessary.

Papa left it in her hands.

"We're down to five candidates, and I'm not very excited about any of them." I picked up the top piece of paper and went over my notes. "They all look good on paper, but there's no..."

"Magical fireworks?" suggested Grenie.

"I'd be willing to settle for a flicker at this point." I sighed and set the paper back down. "All my life, I've trusted that my godmother had some magical foresight about this competition. I was sure that between the christening prophecy and my own system of testing the princes, I would find someone who would be a good match and co-ruler."

"Talking to yourself again, *ma chouchoutte*?" It was Papa. Mother must have sent him to make me rejoin the party.

Grenie casually hopped off the bench with a convincing, "*Ribbit.*"

"Hi, Papa, am I supposed to come and be sociable now?"

"That's what your mother would like." Papa looked me over. "But I don't think it's what you need tonight."

"And what do I need?" I closed my notebook and tucked it into my bag.

"Sugar, flour, and maybe some butter." Papa's eyes twinkled. "Let's go bake."

"We can only be an hour or so," Papa reminded me, glancing at the golden clock on the wall of the Parisian apartment that kept Faerie time. "Or too much time will pass at home and your mother will murder us both."

"I know, Papa. I have just the thing. I started it last time I was here." I pulled up a stool to the marble island and flipped open the laptop.

"The internet?" Papa grumbled. "You know how I feel about recipes from the internet. Anyone can take a nice photo and say it's 'the best chocolate cake ever!' but—"

"But there's no way to know if they have any training. I know. I know." I found the blog I was looking for.

"In my day," he went on, "you had to be a chef to write a recipe."

"In the dark ages, you mean?" In Faerie, everyone aged slower, humans and fae alike. "I'm pretty sure non-chefs wrote recipes back then too. And you didn't have digital thermometers."

Papa kept grumbling, but I ignored him and pulled up the recipe.

"Here. I know this girl isn't a chef, but I've tried a few of her recipes and they've all been amazing."

"Pie in the Sky," Papa read aloud. "Are we making pie?"

"No, that's the name of her blog. And her cafe, I think. Anyway, these are what I have ready to go in the fridge." I tapped the photo.

Papa's face lit up as he read the recipe title. "Ah, Tuala, that's perfect."

"Papa, how did you know mother was the right person for you to marry?" I pulled a bowl of dough out of the gleaming stainless-steel fridge.

"Hmm, well, you know we met here in Paris." Papa handed me an apron, and I tied it on over my dress.

"You were in culinary school, and she was studying painting." I knew this part of the story.

"Correct. And of course, I had no idea that the beautiful girl I saw painting *en plein air* in the park everyday was a faerie princess." Papa checked the temperature on one of his favorite human gadgets, the deep fryer.

"Because she was glamoured, of course." I turned the bowl of dough onto the floured marble island and started rolling it out.

"Of course. But even still, she was enchanting. And whenever we spoke, she made the world light up around her. Not magic…just…" he trailed off, his hands still motioning.

"Love?"

"*Oui.*"

I sighed. "That doesn't really help, Papa." I checked the width of the dough and began cutting it into squares.

"It's not something you can explain, *ma chouchoutte.*" Papa lifted a square of dough and carefully dropped it in the fryer. "And while I'm going along with this silly competition for your mother's sake, it's not something you can test for or make lists to figure out. It's something you feel in your heart."

"That does sound wonderful," I admitted. "But while I wait to feel that *something*, I'll keep making my lists."

"Ah, Tuala, you like to act as if logic rules you, but I know you have a tender heart." He lifted the basket with the first batch of puffed, golden squares out of the fryer and tipped it onto a waiting plate covered with a towel to soak up the grease.

"I do, do I?" I picked up the shaker of powdered sugar and dusted the pile of golden treats. I'd have to sneak one to Grenie. That frog certainly had a sweet tooth.

"Of course you do." Papa carefully dropped the second batch of dough squares into the fryer one at a time. "You are someone who loves with her whole heart. Why else would you have chosen to make the treat your mother has been dreaming of all week?"

"Hmm, I'm not sure how that will help me choose a prince." I dusted my hands off on my apron.

"You will just have to listen to your heart, *ma chouchoutte*." He reached over and hugged me to his side. "Now, let's finish these *beignets* up and make your mother smile."

I hugged Papa back, but I didn't know what good a tender heart would do me, when the only people I wanted to spend time with were my father and a frog.

CHAPTER 8

I LOOKED OVER THE REMAINING CHALLENGERS and felt...nothing. Well, that wasn't completely true. I did feel a bit annoyed when I saw Forlagh, the brownie, hanging around with no sign of the prince from the Juniper Court.

"Trust Clíodhna's wisdom," said my mother in a low voice, noting my discomfort.

"And we can always call this whole thing off," added Papa, with a meaningful look at his wife.

My mother sniffed. "It'll all work out, you'll see."

I envied her confidence. But, I'd come this far, I might as well see it through.

"Congratulations on making it to the final challenge," I told the princes. "This last test is simple. All you have to do—" I raised my hands. "—is find me."

I clapped my hands together and disappeared in a puff of sparkling golden smoke.

When the smoke cleared, I saw that the flashy transportation spell had worked. I'd have to thank the court magician.

My hiding spot was a moss-covered old lookout tower across the moat, on a hill behind the castle. It wasn't far, but we hadn't been here on any of the previous challenges. The only ones who knew where I had disappeared to were the castle servants. The plan was simple. The princes needed to ask a servant about my whereabouts. And they needed to be polite and humble, or the servants would send them on a wild goose chase. I had no interest in marrying a snob, and humility was possibly the most important trait in a ruler.

I arrived outside the tower in a small meadow surrounded by trees. Dark clouds rolled in, and the greens of the trees and grass intensified as a light rain began to fall. I flipped up the hood of my velvet cloak. Good thing my hiding spot came with a roof.

I lifted my linen skirts and started up the tower stairs.

"*Léas*," I murmured. The candles in the wall sconces flickered to life, lighting my path to the top.

A domed roof topped the lookout tower, held up by graceful arches of carved stone. Earlier this morning, the cook had sent a maid with a basket of food, and I was pleased to see she had included a quilt and a couple of cushions. I made a little nest under one of the stone arches and looked out over the castle.

I was too far away to see what the princes were up to, but I laughed when I spotted Cressie rolling around in the moat like a giant scaly otter. The *peiste* loved rainy days.

The rain came down harder. How long would it take for a prince to break down and ask a servant? An hour? Longer?

I opened my bag and pulled out my notebook. All the remaining princes looked good on paper. Any one of them would make a good co-ruler, but I almost wished none of them would find me. Stupid, useless notebook.

I tore the first paper out of the book and folded it into a paper dragon like I used to make as a kid. I sent the list sailing out into the air, watching it soar until the rain soaked it and sent it tumbling down.

Seemed about right. I made five more out of my remaining lists and watched them all fly and then crash. Just like my hopes for these trials.

"You almost hit the moat with that last one."

"Grenie?" I looked back to see the little green frog hopping up. "How did you know where I was?"

"I asked the dark-haired kitchen maid." The frog settled onto the quilt beside me. "Lillian."

"She must have jumped out of her skin," I said with a laugh.

"Nah, she's been sneaking me bits of pastries all week. Speaking of which..." Grenie leapt to the picnic basket. "What do you think she packed for us?"

"For us, eh?" I unfolded the tea towel covering the food.

"I may have mentioned my love for brambleberry turnovers." Grenie peered into the basket. "Feel free to pass me one."

"There's more than brambleberry turnovers in here." I set a sugar-crusted pastry on the quilt and the little frog hopped over to it.

"Oh really?" He took a bite and sighed happily.

"Really." I pulled out a folded piece of thick paper sealed with the crest of the Juniper Court. "I wonder how he knew to send this in the basket."

"Perhaps the prince has also been begging pastries from Lillian?"

"I suppose that's possible." I was surprised at the flash of jealousy it gave me to think of Naven spending time with a maid while avoiding me. I shook my head and examined the note. The back was addressed to me, still in that flowery script. It must be Forlagh's writing. "But why doesn't he write his own letters?"

"Perhaps he is currently without the use of his thumbs," said Grenie through a mouthful of brambleberry.

"Hmmm." I cracked the wax seal and read aloud:

Dear Tuala,
I know you've been frustrated with me this week,

"How does he know that?" I asked my green companion.

"Perhaps he's very observant?" said the frog.

But I assure you, I have been equally frustrated.

"Seems unlikely." I narrowed my eyes at the letter.

"Would you just finish reading the note? It's not even very long." Grenie sounded exasperated. Touchy frog.

When we were children, I know I teased you relentlessly about your godmother's prophecy. But when we danced together at the Beltane Ball, I realized I would do anything to win this challenge.

"He only danced with me once," I told the frog. "I looked for him the rest of the evening."

"Perhaps your very protective father mentioned that you were only sixteen, and that a dedicated suitor would be willing to wait two years."

A tingle ran down my spine, and I kept reading.

I have waited for you. And I have done everything I could to prove my love for you this week. Only your hurt feelings have kept you from declaring me the winner of the first two challenges.

Can you find it in your heart to forgive me, and grant me the prize of this final test?

Yours, Naven.

"How can he be the winner when he's not even here?" I folded up the note again.

"Maybe you're not looking hard enough?" Grenie cleared his throat.

I looked over at him.

He looked back at me.

"Seriously?"

"Did it sound like a humorous letter?" asked the frog.

"You're Naven?"

"*Croak*," he said.

"How am I supposed to believe you?" I picked up the frog and examined it. Looked like a perfectly normal frog. Except for the whole talking thing.

"There's only one way to find out," said Grenie, legs dangling. "If I'm the winner, give me the prize."

"You want to go on a date?" I tried to imagine it. A romantic getaway with a frog. Honestly, it would beat the first two dates.

"I do, but maybe start with the other part of the prize."

I blinked at him.

"I'll just croak if I say it. You'll need to figure it out on your own. What does your mother keep saying?"

"That the only way to tell if someone is your true love...is to kiss them."

The frog tilted its head meaningfully.

Kissing a frog. It didn't make a lot of logical sense. But my logic had crashed into puddles at the base of the tower. Maybe it was time to listen to my heart instead.

Before I could think too hard about what I was doing, I closed my eyes.

And I kissed the frog.

HANNA SANDVIG

CHAPTER 9

A T FIRST, NOTHING HAPPENED. My heart sank. Of course, it was too silly to be true. What had I expected to accomplish by kissing a frog?

Then Grenie started growing bigger and I hastily set him down beside me. A cloud of green mist smelling faintly of pond thickened around the frog, then with a popping sound, it dissipated. And there, in the wisps of green smoke, sat Naven. He looked a bit shocked, running a hand through his thick blond hair, and patting his clothing, as if to check and see if he was really there.

He recovered quickly and turned to me, with a grin. "Tuala. Can we try that again?"

I picked my jaw up off the floor. "I…Try what again?"

Naven leaned forward and tilted my chin up with his hand. "This."

It was a gentle brush of his lips on mine, but it was full of promise, and I found myself leaning in and kissing him back.

And it turned out my mother was right.

This one, said my heart, as I tangled my hands behind his neck, *This is the one we were waiting for.*

When we arrived back at the castle, our hands clasped and unable to stop grinning, my mother actually squealed with glee. We explained everything to my parents and my papa gave us both big bear hugs.

The remaining princes were located and politely informed that the challenge had ended. Only one was headed in the right direction. I supposed he would win points for that, if I hadn't thrown my lists off the tower.

Maybe it was too soon to say if Naven was my true love, but my head agreed with my heart. The rest of the princes didn't stand a chance next to him.

My mother had chosen dinner in Paris as the date for the final challenge. She said that she had fallen in love with my papa there, and while it might be in the human realm, the city contained its own magic. We arrived in mid-afternoon and changed into human clothes to do some exploring before dinner.

"So, have you ever been to France?" I asked Naven.

He looked adorably awkward in jeans and a dark green T-shirt. He fiddled with the gold necklace that cast a glamour to make him pass as human. I wore a matching necklace and a flowered pink sundress.

"I have not." He looked everywhere at once and collided with a tall dark-haired boy holding hands with a girl in a red hoodie. They laughed and she apologized. Her accent said Canadian, which would explain why she said, "Sorry," when Naven was the one who had run into them.

"Have you been to the human realm at all?" I asked as we continued down the street. "Wait, we need to stop here and get macarons. Trust me. It's important." I grabbed the prince's hand and tugged him toward Ladurée.

"I visited New Zealand once with my brother." He adjusted my grip so our fingers intertwined, his pale fingers around my brown ones. "It was nothing like this. This is busier than the Seelie Court. But you come here often?"

I nodded. "My papa said I would never learn French properly if I didn't spend time in France."

We entered the shop and examined the stacked pastel pyramids of macarons. I got a box with some of my favorites, and a chocolate orange one for my mother.

"Why do you need to speak French when you live in Faerie?" Naven took the pastry box from me and reached for my hand with his free one.

"So my parents can't keep secrets from me, of course!"

Later that day, we sat at a little table on a patio overlooking the River Seine. The sun cast a golden spell over the river, and the Eiffel Tower twinkled on the far side as it lit up for the evening.

A waiter brought us a fresh, sliced baguette with delightfully stinky cheese. I took a sip from my glass and laughed.

"Mint tea with honey?" I took another sip and sighed. Perfection.

"Your father asked if there was anything we needed to make the dinner perfect. I think he knows the owner?"

I nodded and poured him a glass as well. "That sounds like him."

After the waiter took our order, I leaned forward. "All right, Naven, it's time to fess up."

"To what?" He took an innocent sip of iced tea.

"You know what. The whole frog fiasco. The amphibian incident. What happened?"

"Oh, that." The prince buttered a piece of baguette. "We were on our way to your challenge. Forlagh was helping me carry my belongings to the Juniper Gate—you might owe him an apology, by the way. None of this was his fault."

"It's true. Poor Forlagh. I'll bake him a cake tomorrow."

"He likes hazelnuts. Anyway, we were about to go through the gate to the Lily Court when out stepped an old woman in a red cloak."

"Who was she?" I took a bite of my own bread, savoring the pungent, gooey cheese on top.

"I don't know. She had the hood pulled down. I could only see the bottom of her face. Anyway, she offered to grant me a wish."

"A random old lady offered you a wish, and you asked to be a frog?" I raised my eyebrows.

"I know it seems strange, but there was something familiar about her... Anyway, no. I did not wish to be a frog. I wished to win the competition. To have you see me as not just a childhood friend."

"Well, that was sweet of you." I bumped my knee against his under the table.

"Thank you. Apparently, I should have been more specific. You should have heard her laughing as she cast the spell. Although, to be fair, you didn't see me as your childhood friend."

"Ooooh. That's true." I took another bite of cheese and thought it over. "It seems a bit excessive, but I can't complain too much. My wish certainly came true."

Naven grinned and captured my hand, lightly kissing the back of it. "So did mine."

EPILOGUE

Six months later.

I SWIRLED ACROSS THE STONE-PAVED courtyard in
Naven's arms. I had chosen a deep pink dress for
our engagement ball, with full skirts and a bodice
with gauzy pale-pink petals like an upturned water
lily.

Naven wore a dark green suit with a pond green
cravat. We both laughed when we saw each other. It
was like a picture of how we met that first day of the
trials. Unlike that day, I had managed to get my tow-

ering golden *croquembouche* to this party without falling in the pond.

"Are you happy, Tuala?" murmured Naven in my ear. "You can still back out before the engagement ceremony tonight."

I put a finger to my cheek and pretended to think about it. The ceremony tonight wasn't as official as a wedding, but hand-fasting in *Tír na nÓg* was still a vow. It started the magical bond between us that would grow stronger after we married.

Naven looked at me nervously and faltered a step in the dance.

"Of course, I'm sure," I said with a laugh. "You're the one I want to spend my life with. Even as a frog, you were better company than anyone else I've known."

Naven still officially lived at the Juniper Court, but in the past six months he had spent more and more time here with me and my parents. And while we learned together about the ins and outs of ruling a faerie court, that spark between us had flamed into love. True love, you might even say, if you wanted to be technical about it.

Naven dropped his arm from around me, but kept his other hand grasping mine. He led me through the twirling crowd of dancers, past my mother who was nursing my baby brother on the sidelines, and out of the tent of twinkling lights to stand by the pond with the Lily Gate.

"Much better," I said, tilting my head up for a kiss.

My prince happily obliged, one hand settling on my waist, the other tangling in my hair.

My lips parted and he deepened the kiss, drawing me even closer to his chest.

"I just think we should say something," whispered a female voice.

I jumped, abruptly breaking the kiss. There, a few feet away on a stone bench, sat a couple. He was dark-haired and pale with an eyepatch covering his left eye. She was very short and obviously very human in a yellow silk ballgown. A small lantern glowed on the back of the bench and both of them had books in their laps.

"I apologize for my fiancée," said the fae man, rising and giving a polite bow. He helped the girl up from the bench. "I told you, *Àlainn*, we should have just crept out. We disturbed them."

"How, Leith? They were blocking the exit. Or do you think we should have jumped the hedge and landed in yet another pond on the other side? That would have been sooo inconspicuous."

The man, Leith, sighed, but he looked at her with a twinkle in his eye.

"Um, and you are?" asked Naven, still blushing from the interruption.

"Oh, sorry." The girl laughed. "I'm Isobel, and this is Leith."

"Prince of the Rose Court, at your service." The man bowed again, still holding Isobel's hand. When we had sent out invitations to the challenge, the reply from the Rose Court had simply read "unavailable." That much was clearly true.

"And you're Tuala and Naven," said Isobel, reaching out to shake our hands. "It's so nice to finally meet you."

"Leith, you have to help me!" Prince Declan burst into the little alcove.

"I clearly need more practice at finding private spots," sighed Naven.

"It's Tiernan." The shaggy-haired prince glanced back in the direction of the party.

"Again?" Prince Leith rolled his eye and followed Declan. "How many hearts can he break in one evening?"

"It was nice to meet you," I called after them. "I think..."

"Oh! Before we go, I have something for you." Isobel patted the hips of her full golden skirts.

"Oh, gifts aren't necessary," I assured her.

"It's not a gift exactly." She pulled a folded piece of paper out of a pocket. "It's a message."

"From who?" I accepted the paper.

"We have a mutual acquaintance. She gave this to me last spring and told me to pass it along when I saw you." She winked and turned to go. "Congratulations on your engagement!"

"What does it say?" Naven leaned over to peek but I led him by the hand to the bench where the lantern still sat.

I unfolded the paper. It felt smooth and thin, clearly from the human world.

Dear Tuala and Naven,

I do hope you'll forgive me for not making it to your engagement party. So long as the Unseelie Queen hunts me, it's best if I don't draw trouble by spending much time in Faerie.

I know your courtship seemed a bit unusual, to say the least, but I also know it has forged a bond between you that will stand the tests of time. And think of the stories you'll tell your children!

Sometimes the path to true love is unconventional, but I know in my heart that you two will truly live happily ever after.

Save me a spot at your wedding!

Your loving Godmother,
Clíodhna

"If Isobel got this note in the spring, that's before the trials even began," mused Naven.

"I'm sure there's a lot to wonder about." I re-folded the note and tucked it into my pocket. "But I don't have any doubts about one part."

"Which part?" Naven kissed my cheek.

I leaned in and whispered in his ear, "That we'll live happily ever after."

He kissed me again, with the twinkling *sheerie* dancing around us on the water, and I smiled against his lips. Never had there been a girl as lucky to fall into a pond as me.

Want to spend more time in Faerie? Try The Rose Gate, a retelling of Beauty and the Beast. This stand-alone novel kicks off the Faerie Tale Romances series, and tells the story of Leith and Isobel, who you met briefly in The Lily Gate!

Or, if you're curious about the couple Tuala and Naven bumped into in Paris, read on for a sneak peek of The Wolf Gate, A retelling of Red Riding Hood, now available.

I

go
the
At
the
nev
upc

sed
ore
t it,
of

: all
my
; at

www.HannaSandvig.com

AUTHOR'S NOTE

MY VERSION OF TÍR NA NÓG is loosely based on Irish folklore. If you'd like to learn more about the world and the faeries that inhabit it, go to my website where you can find a map and a list of the various races with a little bit about each of them.

At my website you can also see illustrations I drew for all the books, and sign up for my newsletter. I use my newsletter to send you updates on my books, peeks at upcoming art, and fun printables.

www.HannaSandvig.com

ACKNOWLEDGEMENTS

THANK YOU TO THE LADIES OF Enchanted Quill Press for putting together the Princess Bachelorette anthology that The Lily Gate was originally written for. It was a fun experience!

Thanks to my incredible beta readers, Sonya, Julie, Kari, Joanna, Rose, Kirsten, Laura, Kathryn, Kadi, Karen, Colleen, Stephanie, Kathy, and my typo hunters, Hannah, Nic, Rebecca, Anna, Sarah, Anne, Danae, Crystal, and Lillian. Thanks to my mom for your wonderful feedback.

Thanks to Becky for your edits. I'll never learn how to use commas.

Thank you to Maru for drawing the sweet illustration of Tuala on the opposite page! You can check out her comic and animation work at: MaruExposito.com

Most of all, thank you to God for your love.

A Faerie Tale Romance Novella

THE
WOLF GATE

a Retelling of Little Red Riding Hood

by

HANNA SANDVIG

CHAPTER 1

"T HAT'S IT." NEVE PULLED MY CUP away from me and hid it behind the bar. "You're cut off."

"Nooooo," I whimpered. "Sweet, sweet nectar, come back to me!"

"Audrey, you've had three cups of coffee. It's eight already. In the evening. You'll be up all night and sending me ridiculous texts at two-thirty in the morning."

"I would never." I gave my best friend my most tragic puppy-dog eyes.

"That's what you said last week." Neve held up her phone.

I pushed my dark-framed glasses up on my nose and examined the screen. It read: *Still can't sleep. Never let me drink coffee again. If you see me drinking coffee, slap it out of my hand. 2:36AM.*

"I was clearly delirious." I leaned back on my barstool. "You've gotten cold in your old age."

"Delirious from sleep deprivation! And if I'm old at seventeen, you must be ancient at eighteen. I'm the picture of youth." Neve pulled open the retro pink fridge behind the bar and peered inside.

"And yet, so heartless."

"Shhh. Have some pie. It's apple ginger." She slid a slice of pie across the polished wood on a floral china plate.

Pie in the Sky, Pilot Bay's finest cafe (okay, only cafe, unless you counted the coffee counter at the gas station), was owned by Neve's parents. Her dad handled the money, and her mom was responsible for the pretty, shabby-chic decor, but everyone knew that it was Neve who was the genius with pastries. Her chocolate cookies could bring boys to their knees. When you added that to her curvy, tattooed, vintage pin-up-girl vibe, she was irresistible. Not that she seemed to care. She said the local boys lacked a certain something. Her aloof attitude only made them love her more.

I, on the other hand, couldn't even get my boyfriend to meet me for coffee.

"I have to close in fifteen minutes. Did Dylan text you back? Is he coming?" My friend pulled out a bandana from her apron pocket and tied her dark hair back. Cleaning mode engaged.

"Nothing. I even promised him free pie." I took a bite of my own pie. So flaky. So perfect.

"Humph, I'm not sure he's worthy of apple ginger." Neve grabbed a cloth and scrubbed the counter aggressively. "I'm sorry. I know you like him. I'm just not sure why."

"Well…it isn't for his punctuality. You do have to admit he's pretty to look at." When he was around. "And the accent is nice."

"Gavin also had that lovely Irish accent, and he was never late." Neve picked up my plate and wiped under it before setting it back down.

"Could we please not talk about my ex-boyfriend? Like…ever?" I took another bite and considered telling Neve the real reason I had asked Dylan to meet me tonight. But while I was still chewing, the cafe's phone rang.

"Hi, Aunt Chloe." Neve tucked the phone between her ear and shoulder and kept cleaning. "Uh

99

huh. I have two chocolate with salted caramel buttercream and six vanilla bean with lavender buttercream." She laughed. "Of course, chocolate always sells better. I can't get away for another hour, though. I still have to clean up and cash out."

I listened with half my attention while finishing my pie and composing a scathing text to my absent boyfriend.

"Oh, yes, she's here. How did you guess?"

I looked up at Neve in surprise. Although maybe I shouldn't have been. Her Aunt Chloe knew everything. No story too big, no gossip too small.

"I'll ask her, just a sec." Neve pulled the phone from her ear. "Audrey, I know you're waiting for Dylan, but would you mind making a delivery for me? Aunt Chloe needs some cupcakes. She's expecting her book club ladies and the one in charge of snacks is sick. It's a dessert emergency."

I glared at my phone and hit send with a sigh. "Fine. If he happens to stop by, tell him I went home. I assume his phone must have gotten run over by a car, or he'd be answering my texts."

"What if Dylan got run over by the car?" Neve moved the glass cover from the cake stand to the counter and carefully boxed her tasty creations.

"Then, I will consider forgiving him." I tucked my phone into my backpack and accepted the pink pastry box from my friend.

"Thank you, Audrey. Come over in the morning and we'll re-dye the ends of your hair, I can barely see the pink anymore."

"Sure, sure." I slid off my stool. Anything to make my pale, freckly blonde self more interesting. Reaching across the bar, I hugged my friend. "Thanks for the pie. See you tomorrow."

The rain I ran through earlier today had stopped, but the sidewalk was still wet and the air felt cool for July. I dodged puddles the size of small lakes as I walked down Main Street on my way to Miss Chloe's house. Yes, Pilot Bay had only one major road through town, and yes, it's called Main Street. You had to give the town fathers props for clarity if not originality. You might have thought that at eighteen I could probably drop the Miss, but sadly, that's impossible. Miss Chloe was Pilot Bay's head librarian, and she'd been shushing me and my friends since we were toddlers.

Miss Chloe was not actually Neve's aunt. They weren't even related. She was more like a godmother if anything, but the Klassens weren't Catholic, so aunt it was.

I cut across the street and past the mishmash of houses—mansions to trailers—on the west end of town, before coming to the dirt road leading to Miss Chloe's house. She lived just beyond the outskirts of town, but the road was pretty, lined with tall pine trees and mossy rocks. It was just starting to get dark out, but I didn't think I'd have any trouble making it home before night fell.

I turned the last bend in the road and there was Miss Chloe's house. It looked like a fairy-tale cottage, with a tall peaked roof. Climbing roses covered the shingled siding around one corner. The windows glowed in the dusky evening light.

I climbed the front steps and knocked on the bright red front door. Instead of the usual lion, her brass knocker was shaped like a bear's head. More appropriate for British Columbia, I supposed.

Miss Chloe poked her curly gray head out the door and smiled when she saw me.

"Audrey, you've saved me. None of the book club ladies were going to get to the bakery in time." She adjusted her gold-rimmed glasses and stepped back into the house. "Come in for a minute. I have something for you to take to Neve."

"Oh, I don't know how much the cupcakes cost," I protested. "I'm just the delivery girl."

"No, no, it's not about money." Miss Chloe waved me in, and I obediently entered. I'd walked over here with Neve before, but I'd never been inside. The entryway was spotless. A gilded mirror hung on the wall, flanked by paintings of roses.

"You'll be seeing her tomorrow, right?" she asked. "For the anime festival in Rossland?"

"Um, yes? I don't know if I'd actually call it a festival." I tugged at the hem of my black Naruto t-shirt. "I'm not sure more than five people in the Kootenays even watch anime. I don't have high hopes."

Miss Chloe just smiled and opened the box of cupcakes, inhaling deeply. "It's going to take all my willpower to wait until the other ladies arrive," she said happily. "Neve's baking improves every day."

I nodded politely, trying not to look too anxious to leave. I didn't actually want to walk home through the woods in the dark.

The older lady shut the pastry box with a sigh and headed into the house. "I'll just find that item for you. Come sit in the living room. Don't worry about your shoes."

I padded after her, having already slipped out of my red chucks. Canadian force of habit. The living room smelled of roses with giant bouquets gracing the mantle and coffee table.

"You sure like roses." I held my backpack on my lap and perched on the edge of the plush couch. It was heaped with pillows which all had—surprise!—embroidered roses on them. Except one. I picked it up, squinting at the beautifully stitched design. Was that Iron Man?

"They're terribly friendly flowers, you know." Miss Chloe opened a wooden chest under the window and rummaged around. "I know it's in here somewhere…"

"I really should be going soon." I looked past her, out the window where the forest was growing darker. "The fastest way home is the trail through the forest, but it—"

"It's getting dark. Yes dear, I know. Ah, here it is." Miss Chloe pulled a long swath of red velvet from the blanket box. She shook it out with an air of satisfaction, and I leaned forward, embroidered Iron Man forgotten, as I saw what she held.

The cloak was gorgeous, with a deep hood and thick folds of scarlet velvet that would fall nearly to the ground if I wore it. Gold thread embroidered the edges in curling, twining designs. A pair of heavy-looking gold clasps held the front together.

Miss Chloe plopped it in my lap, and I found myself petting the plush red fabric. It felt so cozy, and…was it buzzing somehow? I squinted at the embroidery. The golden knotwork pattern seemed to spin in an intricate twisting pattern, growing in depth like fractals around the threads. I shook my head and the glowing pattern faded.

Well, that was weird. Neve had been right to cut off my caffeine. I obviously needed an early bedtime tonight. I folded the cloak up as well as I could before cramming it into my backpack.

"You'd best be heading home." Miss Chloe peered out the window. Daylight was fading quickly now.

I stood, swinging my backpack onto my shoulder with a grunt. The cloak felt heavier than I expected. "What does Neve need a cloak for anyway?"

"Oh, you never know when it might come in handy," Miss Chloe called back over her shoulder as I followed her to the door. She stopped abruptly in the entryway, and I almost ran into her. "Audrey." She examined me through her gold-framed glasses. "I regret not being able to give you more attention."

"Um, that's okay." I had no idea what the librarian was apologizing for. When had she ignored me? "I don't really read all that much."

"You'll do well." She gave my shoulder a reassuring pat. "You're stronger than you realize."

"Thanks?" Should I tell Neve that her aunt was possibly struggling with dementia? "I really should go now, though."

Miss Chloe opened the door and stepped out onto the porch. She glanced up at the sky, purple and cloudy in the twilight. "Good luck, my dear."

"It's only a fifteen-minute walk to my house, Miss Chloe," I said with a laugh as I ran down the stairs. "I'll be fine. Enjoy your book club." I definitely needed to check in with Neve about her.

Pilot Bay was nestled into the mountains with Kootenay Lake on one side and forests surrounding the rest of town. There were trails all around the edges of the community, some leading into the mountains, some creating shortcuts to other neighborhoods. I'd grown up here and I knew the trails as well as the true roads in the area. Halfway back to town from Miss Chloe's, I turned onto a bike trail that would connect to the little path running past my backyard.

It was darker on the smaller trail, with the trees thick around me, but it would take twice as long to walk through town. So, I walked quickly and tried to keep my eyes on the path instead of scanning the trees for the reflective gleam of cougar eyes. No one had seen a cougar around town. This year.

I found the crossroads with no problem and started down the little path to home. It was almost full dark now, but I wasn't worried.

Not until I heard the howl.

I stopped in my tracks. I'd always heard about wolves living in our mountains, but I'd thought I'd have to be lucky to see one, they were so rare. My pulse kicked up at the wolf's howl, but it sounded far away, deep in the woods. For a moment, I listened to the winds whisper through the trees. With a shiver, I started moving again. I'd have to tell Neve I heard a wolf. It'd be a good story.

Then I heard an answering howl and all the hair stood up on my arms. This one was *not* far away. I broke into a jog, scanning the trees, not in the least bit prepared when a large gray wolf bounded onto the path in front of me.

I shrieked, my heart hammering.

Its pale, yellow eyes bore into me. I froze. I couldn't even breathe. Now I could say I'd seen a wolf. I did not feel lucky.

I pivoted in a spray of dirt and bolted from the path into the forest.

This might not have been the wisest move. In my panic, I thought I could hide in the dark forest, but the thing was, the wolves could see in the dark.

And I couldn't.

I crashed along blindly through the undergrowth, my legs getting battered and scraped by unseen branches, the wolf right on my heels. Then I heard a second howl.

Seriously, though? Weren't wolves supposed to be more afraid of me than I was of them?

With a crash and a snarl, a second, darker, wolf caught up to the first and nearly ran it over in its eagerness to eat me first. I tripped in the dark, foolishly focusing on wolves instead of my feet.

The wolves untangled themselves. Two pairs of gleaming eyes watched me climb to my feet.

"N-nice wolves." I held up my hands. "Please don't eat me."

One stepped closer, growling, but the dark wolf lunged for me, snapping at my ankles. I took off through the forest again, even though I knew I would never be able to outrun them.

In fact, I hardly took more than a few steps when one of the wolves crashed into me from the side. I fell beneath its weight. This was going to be the end for me. No more Audrey.

But I was surprised by three things. One, it was suddenly bright out, as bright as midday. Two, instead of falling into a bush, I landed in a snowbank. A snowbank in July. But most surprising of all was the third thing. The heavy weight that pushed me into the snowbank, was not, in fact, a wolf. It was Gavin McKenna, my ex-boyfriend.

Given a choice, I might have chosen the wolf.

About the Author

HANNA SANDVIG IS TURNING YOUR favorite fairy tales into faerie tales with some sweet romance and enough sass to keep things interesting.

Hanna is living out her personal happily-ever-after in the mountains of BC, Canada with her husband, three little girls, and giant cat. When she's not writing, drawing, or reading, she can be found sewing, taking photos, baking, and desperately trying to not pick up any more creative pursuits. If you drop in to visit, please bring plenty of chocolate and strong black tea.